Voyage
of the
Vagabond

Betty Frost

D1293515

A **PERSPECTIVES** BOOK
High Noon Books
Novato, California

Series Editor: Penn Mullin
Cover and Illustrations: Herb Heidinger

International Standard Book Number: 0-87879-296-1

9 8 7 6 5 4 3 2 1
20 19 18 17 16 15 14 13 12

You'll enjoy all the High Noon Books. Write for
a free complete list of titles.

Contents

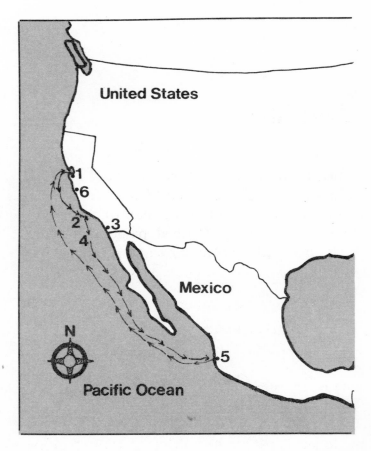

1.San Francisco Bay; 2. Santa Catalina; 3. Santa Barbara;
4. Whales were spotted here; 5. Puerta Vallarta; 6. Monterey.

CHAPTER 1

Bad News

Paul Martin put his shoulder against the boat trailer. Then he shoved it easily across the boat yard. He wiped some paint off his hot face. Then he stood back to look at the hull of the racing yacht. He had just finished painting it blue. After long hours of sanding and scraping, the pretty sloop should now be safe from marine pests for months.

"Looks good, Paul," yelled Hal Wilson. Hal owned the Wilson Boat Yard.

Paul smiled back at his boss. He liked working with Hal. Paul had been a raw kid at the beginning of the summer. Three months later he felt strong and good about himself.

How he had hurt for the first few weeks! Trying to keep up with the tough pace Hal set, every muscle had hurt. Paul had been almost too tired to sleep. Now he was strong and hard. He knew

1

"Looks good, Paul."

he did good work.

Hal had asked Paul to crew on his fast yacht in races on the bay. Here Paul learned racing skills that made him a better sailor. Now he could do the foredeck work. He could set the balloon-like spinnaker from the boat's narrow bow. Then he would handle the heavy lines which worked the sails. He always tried to get the fastest speed.

It had been a great summer. Paul wished it could go on forever. He wanted to keep his job at the boatyard. Then he could save some money for a cruising boat. He and his friends Mike and Joe hoped they could own one some day.

Paul looked at the handsome *Vagabond*. It had been built for Victor and Mary Como. It was a forty-foot-long ocean-going sailboat. Soon the *Vagabond* would be finished. She would move out of this yard and try her wing-like sails across the water. Paul knew he and his friends could never afford anything as fine as the *Vagabond*. But there were other boats. With some money and a lot of work . . .

"Hey, Paul, you were a million miles away," Hal said. "Listen, buddy, I'm going to have to lay some bad news on you. As you know, we don't have as much work here after summer. I'm going to have to cut back. I'm giving you two weeks' notice. Paul, I'm sorry. You've been a darned good worker."

Paul took a deep breath. "I understand, Hal," he said. "Thanks for a great summer. You really taught me a lot."

Paul turned to help launch a beautiful new yacht into the waters of the bay.

CHAPTER 2

Big Changes

Not far from the boatyard, Mary Como hurried up the steps of her house. Her husband, Victor, gave her a big hug. "How was your last day on the job?" Victor asked.

"My friend Marge cried. She said she's going to miss me. We've worked in that kitchen together fifteen years," said Mary. "But I don't mind giving up my job. I wouldn't miss this adventure for anything!"

"It will be a big change, Mary," Victor said thoughtfully. "The galley on the *Vagabond* will seem tiny after the huge hospital kitchen."

"But the *Vagabond's* galley is perfect. It's small, yet it has everything we need," Mary said.

"Let me show you some charts of the coast. I've been studying a possible way south," Victor said.

Mary looked at the charts. She never worried

about sailing when Victor was in charge. He'd been sailing since he was twelve years old. Now he was a great seaman. He could read the wind and the tides. He knew where the shallow water and hidden reefs were.

Victor was also an expert at cabinet work. He had finished the inside of the *Vagabond's* cabin

"I've been studying a possible way south."

himself. For the past two years since he retired, he had spent his weekends at Wilson's Boat Yard. Mary knew that if they hit an ocean storm, Victor could easily repair the *Vagabond*.

"I can't wait to get started on the trip," Mary said.

"I'm proud of you for taking the U.S. Coast Guard course in navigation," Victor told her. "You're going to have to stand some watches when we head south."

"Aye, aye, sir," Mary said. "Right now I'd better fix dinner for the captain."

Victor sat up late that night. He looked at his notebook. Things were going well, he decided. The house should sell easily. There would be plenty of money to finish paying for the *Vagabond* and some left over. Mid-fall would be perfect for the cruise to Mexico. That would be the first part of the voyage.

Victor had to face one problem. He had had a heart attack three years ago. He was fine now. But if he had another attack on the ocean, it would be tough on Mary. Too tough.

Victor reached for the phone and dialed a number. "Hello, Hal. Do you know of a kid who's a good sailor? Mary and I need someone to go with us on the *Vagabond*."

CHAPTER 3

Chance of a Lifetime

Hal Wilson asked Paul to come into his office the next morning. Paul was worried as he sat down. Had he done something wrong the day before?

"I've got some good news for you, Paul," Hal said. "How would you like to sail on the *Vagabond*?"

Paul couldn't believe his ears. The *Vagabond*! The chance of a lifetime! He listened as Hal talked about Mary and Victor's plans.

"It won't pay much," Hal said. "But you would have practically no expenses. And you'll sail along the Pacific!"

"I don't know what to say. The *Vagabond* is a beauty. And the Comos are great people," Paul said. "Let me have a little time to think it over. Thanks a lot, Hal, for giving them my name."

The *Vagabond* was all Paul could think of that

day even though he was busy cleaning up the boat yard. His mind was spinning. Sailing on the *Vagabond* would solve his job problem. And with Victor Como it would be great. The problem was that he had always planned to go on a cruise with Joe and Mike. The three friends had talked of how it would be on a deep water cruise. They would match their skills against the sea. They would go ashore together at strange ports. They would meet new people. Paul liked Mary and Victor. But sailing with them would not be the same.

After work Paul went over to Joe and Mike's house. They lived near the boat yard. It felt good to be with his friends. Comfortable. Fun. They had shared a lot of good times, the three of them. A few rough times, too. They all had long sailing experience. They had rowed miles on the Bay and often swam in its cold waters. Kids learn a lot about the water when they live by the ocean. Skippers who raced always had jobs for them.

And, of course, they all dreamed of a long voyage on their own boat. Paul, Joe, and Mike sat in the kitchen talking about this dream. Paul wasn't sure how to tell them the news.

"Listen, guys, I've got something to tell you. I've been asked to crew on the *Vagabond* to Mexico and —"

"Oh, boy," said Mike, "what a great boat! You are one lucky dude."

"Victor Como is a great sailing man. And his wife can sure cook," Joe added.

"But I always thought we'd do it together. I haven't said I'd go yet," Paul told them.

"Hey, man, no way I can go now," Joe said.

"You are one lucky dude."

"My girl would kill me."

His younger brother, Mike, made a face. "They've got me signed up for a reading course."

"This is your big chance, Paul," Joe said. "Don't let it go by."

Paul saw Victor Como at the boat yard the next morning.

"Hal told me of your offer to sail with you and Mrs. Como," he told Victor. "I would love to do it!"

"Happy to have you aboard!" Victor said. "How about starting off with a tour of the *Vagabond*?"

CHAPTER 4

Heading Out

On a sunny September afternoon Mary Como cracked a champagne bottle on the *Vagabond's* stern.

"I christen thee *Vagabond*," she said. Friends cheered as the handsome boat slid into the bay.

Victor and Paul were already aboard. They set the brand new sails. They checked the standing rigging for strain. They trained store-stiff lines into blocks and around large steel winches. The *Vagabond* was soon properly rigged and "dressed" with little flags. Then Mary came aboard like a queen. The three of them sailed across the Bay. The *Vagabond's* first cruise.

As the days went by, Victor and Paul tested the boat. They sailed on every angle of wind. They changed sails to add or take away sail area. They had to keep in mind the strength of the wind and the height of the seas.

"She handles like a dream boat," Victor said happily.

Then the work of getting supplies for the long voyage began. Food was under Mary's command. Stowed deep inside the *Vagabond* were such things as fresh water, canned goods, dried beans, and pasta. The fresh fruits and vegetables and meats would be eaten first on the trip.

"Mustn't forget these," Victor said. He brought on board two fishing rods. Fresh fish would be a real treat. Bedding, towels, clothing, and rain gear were also packed in the boat.

"Put this in the captain's drawer," Victor said to Paul. He handed him a .22 caliber pistol and a box of ammunition. "We have to rely on ourselves out there on the ocean. I hope we never have to use this."

At last the big day came. The *Vagabond* sailed in the early morning out into the Pacific Ocean. Paul couldn't believe it was happening—at last!

"Say good-bye to San Francisco, Mary," Victor said. "You won't see her again for a long time."

"I'm so excited!" Mary said. "We're really on our way!" She gave Victor a hug.

Victor headed the *Vagabond* down the coast. He was careful to keep away from the rocky shore along the coast. He guided the boat easily over the long ocean swells. The *Vagabond* felt good in his hands.

The weather had turned nasty by mid-morning. There were stiff thirty-knot headwinds. And waves six to eight feet high. Paul went forward to take the jib down. Then he replaced it with the smaller storm jib.

The weather had turned nasty by midmorning.

Mary helped Victor reef the mainsail. She tried to speak but the wind took her words away. She and Victor grinned at each other. Their wet faces shone with salt water.

Paul joined the Comos in the cockpit. He moved very carefully. The boat was rolling wildly.

Victor ordered the lines eased. He headed west into the seas, quartering the waves.

"We'll be in better shape away from land," he said.

The two men were grateful for the mugs of hot soup Mary handed them.

By nightfall the wind had gone down a little.

"Paul, how about taking the wheel for the next four hours?" Victor asked.

"I'll be glad to," Paul said. And he *was* glad.

Soon they were racing along, running before the wind. Hundreds of bright stars dotted the inky black sky.

The *Vagabond* kept sailing south. It was wonderful not to have to stick to a fixed plan. She cruised for several weeks along the islands off Santa Barbara. The weather was perfect, the fishing great. Paul had lots of chances to go ashore. He explored caves and he did some climbing on one island that had a good water supply. The Comos fished for sea bass, bonita, and yellow tail. Paul went scuba diving for abalone and lobster. Delicious meals came out of Mary's tiny galley.

Not far out of San Diego, a pod of about twenty-five whales joined the *Vagabond*. Paul was amazed at how fast they moved. He loved to see them spout as they cleared their lungs.

CHAPTER 5

Emergency Aboard!

"Those are killer or 'grampus' whales," Victor said. "They eat big fish and sometimes even other whales."

Paul felt a chill go down his back. What if one of these twenty-foot whales charged the boat?

On board the *Vagabond* someone was always on lookout now. Just in case.

The wind died. A thick mist settled right to the water's edge.

Victor was on lookout. Suddenly the boat lurched. One of the whales had given the *Vagabond* a sharp bump.

Victor had the boathook out. He was leaning against the mast. He was trying to see in the dim light.

"Paul," Victor shouted, "get the gun!"

Paul was back on deck in a moment with the pistol. Mary was right behind him.

"Oh, no! I've shot him!"

"I don't want you to hit one," Victor said. "The last thing we need is an angry wounded whale. Now listen to me. Load the gun. Then aim it straight into the water. The noise may keep them away from the boat."

Paul fired three shots. With the last blast, Victor fell forward into the cockpit.

"Oh, no! I've shot him!" Paul cried.

Mary's face went pale. "No, no, it's his heart," she gasped. She bent over her husband and rolled him onto his back. She tilted his head to be sure the air passage was open. Next she breathed four quick breaths into his mouth. She then started CPR (cardiopulmonary resuscitation procedure). Thank heavens she had taken the CPR course at the hospital. She had known that someday she might have to save Victor's life.

Paul tested the helm. The *Vagabond* sailed smoothly. No drag. The shots had scared off the whales. The mist cleared. There was a gentle steady breeze.

"I'll help you, Mary," Paul said. "I've been watching you. I think I see how you do it. You count the rhythm for two rescuers. It works better than one. I'll come in on the count of three."

The two worked together. Mary gave one breath, Paul five chest compressions. Color returned to Victor's face. Now he could breathe on his own. The pupils of his eyes were not enlarged. The pulse was getting steadier now.

"P-pills," Victor whispered.

Mary went below to get the heart medicine.

After they had put Victor in his bunk, Paul studied the charts.

"We can be in Mexico at Puerta Vallarta by

tomorrow morning, Mary," he said. "Let's put on the diesel motor for extra speed."

Mary nodded. She sat by the cabin door, looking sadly out to sea. So much was on her mind. She was thinking about Victor and this voyage on the *Vagabond*. They had worked so long and so hard for it. And now this. Victor just had to be kept quiet until they reached Puerta Vallarta in the morning. Paul was young. But he knew how to handle the *Vagabond*. He would get them there. Victor trusted him. She trusted him. He would get there safely. Mary closed her eyes and stayed by Victor.

CHAPTER 6

The Challenge

Paul guided the *Vagabond* to a berth in the Puerta Vallarta harbor. Mary had radioed ahead about Victor's heart attack. How lucky that she spoke Spanish! She could tell the doctors what was needed. An ambulance was waiting at the dock. Victor and Mary were taken to a nearby hospital.

The doctors said Victor would need many weeks of bed rest. Mary was worried, she told Paul.

"I'd feel better if Victor were in San Francisco at St. Stephen's Hospital where I know so many doctors. I don't know what to do."

"Could I go see Victor with you today?" Paul asked.

"Of course, you may," Mary answered.

Victor looked thin and old as he lay in his hospital bed. Paul tried not to show the worry he was feeling about Victor and the trip.

"I miss the boat chow," Victor joked, "but they treat me well here. I think Mary is getting lonely for the big city, though. We're going to fly back. Do you think you can skipper the boat home, Paul?"

"You can count on me, Victor," Paul said.

"I knew I could. Now here is what I want you to do. Find yourself a crew. Should be lots of good sailors around a port like this. Bring the charts tomorrow. We'll plan a northerly course for you."

"You'd better rest now or the doctors will scold all of us," Mary said.

By the end of the week Victor and Mary were gone. Coming back from the airport, Paul felt so alone. And scared. The fate of the *Vagabond* was now in his hands. Would he be able to find a crew?

Paul went down to the dock to check on the *Vagabond*. The waterfront was full of excitement today. It was a holiday. Everyone was in a good mood. Yachts from all over the world were in the harbor.

"Hello, amigo," said a hearty male voice. "I hear you lost your captain and his lady. Too bad."

"Yeah," Paul said, "they are fine people. It's tough luck."

"Luck can change, man. I, Marc Raymond, have seen a lot of blue water over the years. People come, people go. But the sea, she is always there. A man learns how to handle the sea. Then he doesn't want any other life."

"Would you like to come aboard the *Vagabond*?" Paul asked Marc.

"She's something!" Marc said as Paul showed him the boat.

"I worked my passage from Panama on that beauty over there," Marc said. He pointed to a seventy-foot motor sailer. "This is her home port. The end of the line for me."

"I'm looking for crew to take the boat back home to San Francisco," Paul said.

"I like your ship. And I'd like to see Frisco again. Let me think about it. Maybe I'll sail with you," Marc said. He waved and walked off down the dock.

After Marc left, Paul went for a walk along the water. He felt lonely. It was hard being away from home on a holiday. Along the docks, people had pooled their supplies to make a feast. Bands played lively music. The music and singing just seemed to make Paul feel worse. Everyone else is having a great time, he thought. Then he saw a pretty girl sitting alone on a bench. She sat very still, staring into the water.

"Hi," Paul said, "you look about as cheerful as I feel."

"Sorry," the girl said. "It's a funny time to be without your friends and your boat."

Paul introduced himself.

The tall, slim young woman brushed her wavy hair away from her cheek. "I'm Laurie Thomson," she said. "I had shipped aboard as crew and assistant cook in Florida with a neat family. We sailed up from Panama but hit some rocks down the coast. The boat is in drydock there for major repairs. My captain and his family flew home to New York. I decided to come on up to Puerta Vallarta. I like Mexico. I wanted to see more of it. Now I guess I'm just plain homesick."

Paul told her about the Comos and Victor's heart attack.

"A lot of people think cruising is just for the rich," he said. "But Mary and Victor sold their home to pay for the *Vagabond*."

"Many families feel they can't afford to sail," Laurie agreed. "It takes a lot of money to buy a boat like the *Vagabond*. On our trip we met

23

cruising people from all over the world. Some worked their way by taking whatever shore jobs they could get. I've been waiting on tables at the Beach Cafe."

"I worked in a boat yard back home," Paul said. "I could probably help take care of some of these big yachts if I wanted a job."

The couple walked along the docks together.

The couple walked along the dock together.

The whole area was like a giant potluck supper. Everyone had something delicious to share. Laurie and Paul had fun tasting new dishes and talking to the boat people. Later Paul made coffee in the *Vagabond's* galley. Laurie liked the boat. She tested the winches. She liked the inside of the *Vagabond*—its crew quarters, neat dining area, and good space for equipment.

When Paul asked Laurie to sign on as crew, she agreed. She liked the ship and Paul would make a good skipper. They began to make plans for the long voyage to San Francisco. There was so much to do to get the *Vagabond* ready for the trip.

CHAPTER 7

The New Crew Member

Marc Raymond came down to the dock the next day. Paul and Laurie were on board the *Vagabond*. They were washing off her deck.

"Hi, Marc!" Paul called. "Want to grab a sponge and give us a hand? This is a great way to get to know the *Vagabond*!"

"No thanks. Not today. I'll have plenty of time to do that later on. I've decided to sail with you up to Frisco," Marc said.

"Great!" Paul jumped off the *Vagabond* onto the dock. He shook Marc's hand. "That's terrific news. And here's Laurie Thomson, Marc. She'll be sailing with us, too."

Laurie joined them on the dock. She and Marc shook hands. "Did you sail here to Puerta Vallarta?" she asked.

"Yes. I sailed up from Peru. The boat I came on has already left. I wanted to stay around here awhile longer," Marc said.

Peru? Something was wrong. Paul knew it. Hadn't Marc told him he had sailed up from Panama? Hadn't Marc pointed out the seventy-foot motor sailer just last night?

"I thought you said you came up from Panama," Paul said to Marc.

"Panama? Did I say that, amigo? No, it was Peru. I sailed up here from Lima, Peru," Marc said.

"You told me you came on that boat over there," Paul added. He pointed to the seventy-foot model.

"No. Not that one. There was another one right beside it. She pulled out just last night." Marc didn't look at Paul as he spoke.

I don't like this, Paul said to himself. I *know* Marc told me that was his boat last night. And I'm *sure* he said he came up from Panama. If only there were some way to check up on Marc before the voyage. Maybe he should just play it safe and tell Marc to forget the trip. Still, Paul knew he was lucky to have found a crew for the *Vagabond*. He knew he could never sail her home alone.

Maybe he was wrong about Marc. After all, it was dark last night when Marc pointed out the seventy-footer. There was still time left before the *Vagabond* had to leave for San Francisco. Maybe he could find out more about Marc between now and then. But something was giving Paul an uneasy feeling. What it was he wasn't sure yet. But it was there.

"Laurie, I feel like going for coffee," Paul said. "We've worked long enough on this deck. Want to come along, Marc?"

"Sure," Marc answered. "I'll lead the way, amigos."

Paul locked the *Vagabond's* cabin. Then the three of them walked down the dock. They headed for Sam's. It had great coffee and a good view of the harbor.

Sam's was crowded that morning. Paul, Laurie, and Marc found a table in the corner. They all ordered coffee.

Marc started talking about all the boats he had sailed on.

"You've really been around," Laurie said. She slowly sipped her hot coffee.

"You name the place, I've been there," Marc told them. "But Puerta Vallarta is like home."

Paul didn't say much. He mostly listened. He wanted to find out more about Marc. That uneasy feeling was still there.

Suddenly Marc stared at the doorway. His eyes had a scared look. He stopped talking.

"Is something wrong, Marc?" Laurie asked.

"No. It's nothing." Marc kept looking down at the table. Then his eyes moved to the doorway. There was a man standing there. He was staring at Marc. Paul didn't like the way the man looked. The man didn't look like a dock worker. He wore city clothes.

"Got to go now," Marc said suddenly. He jumped up from the table. He quickly walked outside and the man followed him.

"I wonder what happened," Laurie said. "Marc sure looked scared."

"He sure did," Paul agreed. "I wonder if we'll ever see him again. Maybe it would be better if we didn't. I don't feel good about Marc. It's a long way up to San Francisco on the *Vagabond*. We'd be far from shore. A lot could go wrong."

"But a lot could go wrong if just two of us try to sail the *Vagabond*," Laurie added.

"You're right. We can't do it alone. But still, I don't like it. There's something about Marc . . ."

"Maybe we're worrying too much," Laurie smiled. "First, let's see if he shows up at the *Vagabond* again."

"Maybe you're right," Paul sighed. He paid the check and they walked back to the boat.

CHAPTER 8

The Mystery Package

The *Vagabond* had been at sea for four days. It was mid-January. Off the coast of Mexico the weather was warm, the winds gentle. The course was set. Just a short stop for supplies, then they would leave this shelter and move out into the Pacific.

Marc had been signed on as first mate after all. He had come back to the *Vagabond* many times since the day at Sam's. He had helped Paul and Laurie work on the boat. Paul made up his mind to take a chance on Marc. He hoped he wouldn't be sorry.

There had been a farewell send-off for the *Vagabond* at Puerta Vallarta. Marc had come aboard late the next morning. He looked ill. He spent the next two days in his bunk. Paul and Laurie had to handle the ship without him. Fortunately, the going had been easy.

"This is a pleasure cruise for sure," Paul said.

"Enjoy it while it lasts," Laurie kidded. "Wait till we turn the corner into the big ocean. Then the wind can be right down our teeth."

"I know. I've been checking all the rigging. Glad we bought some new line at Puerta Vallarta. There's a lot of wear and strain on rope on a voyage," Paul said.

"Amigos, can you spare a little coffee for an old shipmate?" Marc asked. He poked his head out the hatch.

"You feeling any better?" Paul asked.

"Saying goodbye can take a lot out of a man," Marc said. "Now we are with our mother, the sea. So all is right with the world."

Heading north well off the coast, the going was smooth. But the weather station on the ship's radio reported storms building up. Paul remembered Victor's advice. He headed out to sea so they would miss the rough water near shore. But the hurricane surprised him. He had thought it was too early in the season for one. The sturdy *Vagabond* was tossed like a toy. She went skimming on the tops of the waves. She dove into deep valleys between waves where all one could see was water. Rising to the crests, the spray hit them like a handful of ice cubes. The wind tossed the water across the ship in sheets. Everyone was soaked. Paul made the crew wear life vests.

Paul and Marc worked hard to keep the *Vagabond* steady. They didn't dare turn the boat. They knew the cockpit would fill with water. Laurie spent a lot of time working the pump. When it got stuck, they bailed with buckets for two hours. No one had much rest and tempers were short. Marc complained all the time.

Laurie went below to fix some food for the crew. Suddenly a huge wave hit. The galley cabinet door flew open. Food spilled out onto the galley deck. As Laurie bent to pick things up, another wave caught the *Vagabond*. It shook the stout ship to the port side. Laurie fell into the middle of the mess. She hit hard on one knee and elbow. Just bruises, she decided, as she got up. She started to put everything away again. Far back in the big cabinet she felt something strange. She pulled out a package neatly wrapped in waterproof fabric. What could it be? She tucked the package under the mattress of her bunk. There would be time to think of that later. Right now all that mattered was a good hot meal.

They rode out the storm during the night. Next morning the sky was pale blue, the sun cool. The

Far back in the big cabinet she felt something strange.

crew got a chance to clean up the ship. Scattered lines were neatly coiled. Bedding was aired. When Laurie moved her mattress to dry it, she remembered the mysterious package.

Marc was snoring in the forepeak. No wonder. The *Vagabond* had needed all hands on deck for thirty-six hours.

"Why don't you get some sleep, Laurie?" Paul asked. "In a while," Laurie said. "I'm kind of keyed up now and I want to talk."

"That sounds good to me," Paul answered. "Get a windbreaker and join me. I'm setting a compass course toward Monterey."

Laurie put on her jacket. She put the strange package in her pocket. She told Paul where she had found the package. They decided someone had hidden it there on purpose. Could that someone be Marc? Marc had turned out to be a disappointing crew mate. He was lazy and never talked much.

Neither Paul nor Laurie could imagine what the package contained.

"Put the darned thing in the captain's drawer. And let's keep an eye on that guy," Paul said.

CHAPTER 9

Close Call

The long journey was almost over. Only a few more hours and the *Vagabond* would be passing into San Francisco Bay.

Marc's mood had changed from sulky to mean in the last few days. Now he was crashing around in the cabin. He was overturning cushions, rattling dishes, and throwing life jackets. Only a little while longer and Marc would go his own way. Perhaps he would find some buddies along the San Francisco waterfront, Paul thought.

Laurie was at the wheel. Because they were coming home, Paul wanted the *Vagabond* to look her best. He was facing astern and sanding the wood trim at the edge of the cockpit. Then he would put on a second coat of varnish.

Marc's angry face showed up in the companionway.

"Now you foolish children have made a bad

mistake. You have messed around in something that does not concern you. Now you will pay," he said in a cruel voice.

"He has a knife!" Laurie screamed.

Paul spun around. He leaped for the companionway, grabbing the top of the door frame with both hands. He swung his whole body forward. His heavy sea boots hit Marc full in the chest. The older man fell back into the cabin. He cracked the back of his head on the exposed mast. Paul was on top of him, pinning his arms to the cabin floor. He got Marc's right arm in a hammerlock hold and hung on. Finally the pressure on Marc's right hand was too much. He relaxed for an instant. Then Paul grabbed the knife with his left hand. He tossed the sharp dagger onto the closest bunk. Keeping the hammerlock hold, he yelled for Laurie.

"I need your help here! Set a course and secure the helm."

Laurie obeyed quickly. Then she went below.

"I want to put him in the forward cabin," Paul said.

It took both of them to lift the muscular man, even though he was still groggy. Little by little they moved Marc toward the bow of the ship. At last Paul got a firm hold of Marc's shirt. With

The older man fell back into the cabin.

one good push they got into the forward cabin. While Paul bolted the thick door, Laurie went to the radio.

She put a call through to the U.S. Coast Guard. She told them that there was a violent and dangerous man on board the *Vagabond*. The ship itself was all right though, she reported. The *Vagabond* was asked to put into the Coast Guard

Station just inside the Bay. Laurie agreed.

Meanwhile Paul was back on the helm. He asked Laurie to help trim sails. They tried to ignore the noisy pounding coming from the forepeak. Mark was kicking, punching, and yelling. But the thick door held.

"Thanks, Laurie," Paul said over the noise. "You were great. You really kept your cool."

"You were the one who was great," Laurie answered. "I was scared to death."

Paul looked at Laurie for a minute. He was thinking about Mary and Victor and everything that had happened in Puerta Vallarta and on the way home. He was thinking about Marc. And he was thinking how good it had been that he had met Laurie.

"What a trip this has been," he said.

"A lot has happened," she said and then smiled.

"You know, Laurie," he said. "Someday, somehow, I would love to own my own boat. There are so many places I'd like to go in a boat just like the *Vagabond*."

"I would, too," she said.

"I wonder if owning a boat like the *Vagabond* is just a dream. Could it ever happen?" he asked.

"Anything can happen. Just keep your dreams and work hard," she said.

A Coast Guard cutter met the *Vagabond* and took her to a dock close by in the Bay.

Five Coast Guardsmen came aboard the *Vagabond*. With Paul's permission they entered the cabin. They opened the door to the forward quarters. It took two to hold back the still angry Marc Raymond. They handcuffed him. Then they took him through the cabin to the cockpit. He was put in the patrol wagon waiting on the dock.

In the office of the station commander, Paul and Laurie told him how Marc had been acting. Paul gave the mysterious package to the commander.

An intelligence officer rushed in.

"That guy you brought in on the *Vagabond* belongs to a drug smuggling gang. He's not the big fish, but he's part of it," he said.

The package was opened by the officials. It contained a large quantity of drugs from the Middle East.

"No wonder he was willing to fight for it. It must be worth $150,000," the officer said. "Say, a citizens' group has put up a reward for the capture of anyone involved in a drug ring. Looks like that reward should go to you, Paul! It should be around $5,000," said the station commander.

"I couldn't have done it without Laurie's help," Paul said. "I want her to share in any reward."

"You two can settle that between you," the officer smiled. "I'll turn in your names to the citizens' group that has put up the award. I'm sure you will hear from them. They may want to have a big party and give you the check then."

Paul and Laurie grinned at one another. "Sounds like fun," Paul said.

CHAPTER 10

Back Home

Once again on the *Vagabond*, Paul and Laurie knew that the voyage was almost over. They sailed for the dock at Wilson's Boat Yard. Hal Wilson, a big smile on his face, caught the bow line. He fastened it to a piling. Mary and Victor Como were there to welcome them, too. Paul was happy to see how well Victor looked.

"You've been taking good care of the skipper, Mary," Paul said.

She smiled, "We're very lucky, Paul."

Mike and Joe were also there at the dock. They were all over the *Vagabond*, asking questions.

"Now that you're a real deep water man, you can tell us all about it," Joe said. "I've saved a little money to put into a boat. It's like we always said, the three of us sailing off together."

"I'd love to go again," Paul agreed. "But only if Laurie goes, too. She's too good a shipmate to leave behind."

"You know," Hal Wilson said, "there comes a time when you've got to stop talking about a dream and start moving. Have you guys ever thought about building your own boat?"

Victor and Mary Como smiled. They knew what Hal was thinking. And he was one of the best shipbuilders on the coast.

"Well," Paul said, "I guess that would cost a lot less money than buying one."

"It sure would. And it would be fun, too," Hal said. "Things are still slow here, so you could use my tools. And I could get you a good price on lumber."

Paul looked at Laurie. "You know, Laurie. Half of that reward is yours. I get $2500 and you get $2500."

"Paul," Laurie said, "you were the one who took care of Marc and got us back here. You saved Mary and Victor's boat, not me."

"Without you," Paul said, "I couldn't have done it. Half of that reward is yours."

"I'll take it, Paul, only if I can work with you, Mike, and Joe on the boat. Is that OK, Hal?" she asked.

"Laurie, you sure can. You know more about boats than most people anyway," Hal answered.

"OK, then. It's a deal!"

"OK, then. It's a deal!" Paul said. "We have money to get started."

"And Mike and I will work as our part of the boat," Joe said.

"I have money saved up, too," Mike said.

"Then it's a four-way deal," Paul said.

"Can we help by doing some of the work?" Mary asked. "We could never pay you in money,

Paul, for saving the *Vagabond*, but we can help with some of the work."

"You sure can," Paul answered. "Is it OK, Hal?"

"Well, I think we can work it all out. I'll need some help anyway, so you could give me a hand when I need it. OK?" he asked.

"All right, everyone. It's time for some chow. Come on over to our place, all of you," Mary said.

As they all got into Victor's van, Laurie said, "Paul, so many things happened to us that were surprises, I think we should name the new boat we're-all going to build *The Surprise*. What do you think? Do you like it?"

"Like it? I *love* it!" he answered.